GRAPHIC SCIENCE

A JOURNEY INTO ADAPTATION

WITH

SUPER SCIENTIST

4D An Augmented Reading Science Experience

by Agnieszka Biskup | illustrated by Cynthia Martin and Barbara Schulz

Consultant:
Dr. Ronald Browne
Associate Professor of Elementary Education
Minnesota State University, Mankato

CAPSTONE PRESS
a capstone imprint

Graphic Library is published by Capstone Press,
1710 Roe Crest Drive, North Mankato, Minnesota 56003.
www.mycapstone.com

Library of Congress Cataloging-in-Publication Data is available on the Library of Congress website.

ISBN: 978-1-5435-5869-2 (library binding)
ISBN: 978-1-5435-6002-2 (paperback)
ISBN: 978-1-5435-5879-1 (eBook PDF)

Summary: In graphic novel format, follows the adventures of Max Axiom
as he explains the science behind adaptation.

Art Director and
Designer
Bob Lentz and
Thomas Emery

Cover Artist
Tod Smith

Colorist
Michael Kelleher

Editor
Christopher Harbo

Photo Credits
Capstone Studio: Karon Dubke, 29, back cover;
Shutterstock: Agnieszka Bacal, 7, AridOcean, 8, Isabelle OHara, 25, nattanan726, 14

1 **Ask an adult to download the app.** Capstone 4D Education

2 **Scan any page with the star.**

3 **Enjoy your cool stuff!**

OR

Use this password at capstone4D.com

adapt.58692

TABLE OF CONTENTS

Using bushes for cover, Super Scientist Max Axiom begins his adventures in adaptation from his own backyard.

I'm always amazed by the wonders of nature.

For the animals that live here, my backyard serves as their habitat.

It provides the food, water, and shelter they need to survive.

4

But wings are not this hawk's only adaptation. Its feathers also help it fly and stay warm.

Its excellent eyesight, sharp claws, and curved beak help the hawk catch and kill the small animals it eats.

Together, all of these adaptations help the hawk survive in its habitat.

FLYING SQUIRREL

ACCESS GRANTED: MAX AXIOM

It's a bird! It's a plane! It's a squirrel? The flying squirrel has a fold of skin connecting the wrists of its front legs to the ankles of its back legs. This fold of skin helps the squirrel glide from tree branch to tree branch. With a good jump, flying squirrels can glide 20 to 30 feet through the air.

Of course, the study of adaptation is nothing new.

Hello, Mr. Darwin. Are you going to explore that island?

Let's visit with Charles Darwin. Some important ideas about adaptation were born out of a famous sea voyage he took in the 1830s.

Yes. It's one of the Galapagos Islands. I'm collecting many specimens, including birds, to take back to England.

GEOGRAPHY

The Galapagos Islands are 600 miles west of Ecuador, a country in South America.

Darwin later realized that the finches on the Galapagos had beaks that were adapted to the island food they ate.

Darwin believed that the special beak types developed over the course of many, many years.

Actually, most animals need many generations to adapt to their environments. Rapid changes in an environment make survival very difficult.

The dinosaurs found this out the hard way 65 million years ago.

The meteorite's impact threw huge amounts of dust and ash into the air. This debris blocked out the sun's light and temperatures fell.

KA-BOOM!

Why did the dinosaurs go extinct? No one knows for sure. But some scientists believe that the climate changed quickly after a meteorite the size of a mountain hit earth.

The body features, or physical adaptations, of plants and animals often relate to the environments they live in.

For example, a camel's hump is an adaptation for desert life. When food and water are scarce, the camel uses fat stored in its hump for energy.

The camel's long eyelashes and fuzzy ear hair protect its eyes and ears from blowing sand.

CREOSOTE BUSH

BARREL CACTUS

Plants also cope with dry desert conditions. Since plants lose water through their leaves, the creosote bush has adapted. Its leaves have a waxy coating to help the plant hold in water.

In many cases, plants lack leaves altogether. The barrel cactus stores water in its fleshy stem.

FENNEC FOX

ACCESS GRANTED: MAX AXIOM

Is fur a good adaptation for the desert? For the fennec fox it is. This fox's fur keeps it warm at night when the desert is cold. During the day, the light colored fur reflects sunlight to help keep the fox cool.

Adaptations are not only about physical features. The way animals behave helps them survive too.

For instance, a porcupine thrusts out its quills when it feels threatened.

YELP!

The hognose snake becomes a great actor when threatened. First it pretends to twist with pain. Then it turns upside down, throws back its head, opens its mouth, and sticks out its tongue.

Why does it behave this way? It plays dead because most predators prefer to catch their prey alive.

Along with predators, animals also face harsh conditions in their habitats.

Mice, squirrels, skunks, and bears live in areas where food is scarce during long winters. To survive they hibernate.

During hibernation, animals go into what appears to be a deep sleep.

MAX AXIOM

Animals that hibernate slow down their body functions. Their heart and breathing rates slow. They don't eat for weeks or months. They live on fat stored in the body.

ADAPTATION

Not all flowers smell sweet. In fact, the flowers of the rafflesia plant have adapted to smell just like rotten meat. They give off the horrible smell to attract flies. The flies then carry the rafflesia's pollen to other flowers.

The mimic octopus is a master of mimicry. By changing its shape and color, it can look like sole fish, sea snakes, or lionfish. Scientists believe the octopus developed its mimicry skills because its normal habitat doesn't allow it many places to hide from predators.

Some tube worms, crabs, and clams live at the bottom of the ocean without sunlight or plant life. These animals have adapted to feed on bacteria that grow on the sulfur-rich chemicals spewing from active underwater volcanoes.

Keeping clean is an important behavioral adaptation. Many animals increase their chances for survival by grooming themselves and each other. Monkeys comb through each other's fur, picking off dirt and bugs that might spread disease. Birds preen their feathers to remove bugs and to keep their feathers in first-rate shape for flight.

The Venus flytrap is famous for its ability to trap and digest insects that land on its leaves. This carnivorous plant has adapted to eat insects because the poor soil it lives in doesn't provide enough nutrients.

Bald rockcod have adapted to the freezing temperatures in the Antarctic Ocean. These fish have chemicals in their bodies that work just like antifreeze does in a car. The chemicals keep the fish from freezing solid in the frigid water below the Antarctic ice shelves.

The North American wood frog has adapted to arctic winters by using an extreme form of hibernation. In winter, the frog goes into a deep sleep. Its heartbeat and breathing slow to a stop. Amazingly, much of its body freezes solid. In spring, the wood frog's body thaws and its breathing and heartbeat restart.

BEST BEAKS

Birds have beaks that are adapted to the way they eat. Try this activity to find out which type of bird beak works best for different types of food.

WHAT YOU NEED:

- Internet access
- paper and pencil
- 3 plastic cups
- straw
- tweezers
- pliers
- 3 small bowls
- water
- kitchen timer
- potting soil
- scissors
- yarn
- sunflower seeds

WHAT YOU DO:

1. Use the Internet to look up pictures of a hummingbird, a robin, and a grosbeak. Study each bird's beak and write down how you think it uses it to eat.

2. Place three plastic cups in a row before you. Each cup represents a bird's stomach. Place a straw next to one cup, a tweezers next to the second cup, and a pliers next to the third cup. These tools represent bird beaks.

3. Fill a bowl with water.

4. Set a timer for 30 seconds. Then start the timer and use the straw to move as much water as you can from the bowl to a plastic cup.

5. Repeat step 4 with the tweezers and the pliers, and the other two cups.

6. Compare the amount of water in the three cups and write down which "beak" worked best for moving water. Then empty and dry all three cups.

7. Fill a bowl with potting soil. Cut 20 or 30 2-inch (5-centimeter) pieces of yarn and bury them in the potting soil.

8. Time yourself for 30 seconds as you use each tool to dig out pieces of yarn and place them in the cups. When finished, compare and write down which "beak" collected the most "worms." Then empty all three cups.

9. Fill a bowl with sunflower seeds. Once again, time yourself for 30 seconds as you use each tool to pick up, break, and place sunflower nuts in the cups. When finished, compare and write down which "beak" collected the most nuts.

10. Review your notes from the experiment. Then write down any observations you have about which of your "beaks" best matches the beaks of a hummingbird, a robin, and a grosbeak.

DISCUSSION QUESTIONS

1. On page 9 Max highlights the beaks of three finches on the Galapagos Islands. Why does each finch have a different type of beak? How does each beak help each finch survive?

2. Some scientists think a meteorite strike changed earth's climate and caused the dinosaurs to die out. What other theories have you heard for why the dinosaurs went extinct? Which one do you think is most likely and why?

3. What are the similarities and differences between physical and behavioral adaptations? Give examples of each.

4. Max says that plant and animal adaptations can be seen in our backyards. What are some adaptations you see in plants and animals in your area? Which ones are the most amazing?

WRITING PROMPTS

1. What do you think is the most interesting adaptation Max observes in his travels? Write a paragraph describing that adaptation and explain how it helps the plant or animal survive.

2. Think about a pet, such as a dog, cat, or fish, that lives in your home or a friend's home. Make a list of all of the adaptations that animal has that would help it survive in the wild.

3. Pick a physical adaptation you wish you could have, such as wings, gills, or claws. Write a short story about what you would do with your unique adaptation.

4. What's your favorite animal? Draw a picture of it and label the adaptations that help it survive.

TAKE A QUIZ!

bacteria (bak-TIHR-ee-uh)—very small living things; some bacteria cause disease

camouflage (KAM-uh-flahzh)—coloring or covering that makes animals, people, and objects look like their surroundings

carnivorous (kar-NIV-ur-uhss)—to eat meat; the Venus flytrap is one type of carnivorous plant

climate (KLYE-mit)—the usual weather in a place

extinct (ek-STINGKT)—no longer living anywhere in the world

generation (jen-uh-RAY-shuhn)—the average amount of time between the birth of parents and that of their offspring

habitat (HAB-uh-tat)—the place and natural conditions where an animal lives

hibernate (HYE-bur-nate)—to spend winter in a deep sleep

migration (mye-GRAY-shuhn)—the regular movement of animals as they search different places for food

mimic (MIM-ik)—to copy the look, actions, or behaviors of another plant or animal

predator (PRED-uh-tur)—an animal that hunts and eats other animals

prey (PRAY)—an animal hunted by another animal for food

reproduce (ree-pruh-DOOSE)—to breed and have offspring

specimen (SPESS-uh-muhn)—a sample that a scientist studies closely

READ MORE

Battista, Brianna. *Why Do Pitcher Plants Eat Bugs?: And Other Odd Plant Adaptations.* Odd Adaptations. New York: Gareth Stevens Publishing, 2018.

McAneney, Caitie. *Flying with Feathers and Wings.* How Animals Adapt to Survive. New York: PowerKids Press, 2018.

Spilsbury, Richard, and Louise Spilsbury. *Amazing Animals.* Zap! Mankato, Minn.: Book House, 2018.

Tarakson, Stella. *Stinky Animals.* Gross and Frightening Animal Facts. Broomall, Penn.: Mason Crest, 2018.

INTERNET SITES

Use Facthound to find Internet sites related to this book.

Visit *www.facthound.com*

Just type in 9781543558692 and go!

Check out projects, games and lots more at
www.capstonekids.com

INDEX